I0726326

BEST SERVED SEARING

A FANTASY NOVELLA

JONATHAN EVAN HUDSON

Copyright © 2026 by Jonathan Evan Hudson

All rights reserved.

No part of this book may be reproduced in any form or by any electronic or mechanical means, including information storage and retrieval systems, without written permission from the author, except for the use of brief quotations in a book review.

 Formatted with Vellum

BEST SERVED SEARING

CHAPTER 1
ACE DE SABER

To die in a duel for honor was one thing. To die in a duel to save someone was another.

To die in a duel for both ... no, not his style, dying. The other guy would do all the dying today. After all Ace de Saber wasn't just another out-of-luck prince without a kingdom in the whole entire world of Trifacto, he had friends and family, all who cared for him, and cared deeply.

None of that ridiculous royalty crap.

So time to prove his training true, Trained by the best to be the best.

Time for Ace to face that wannabe swordsman of the wood elf race. A wiry twig of a boy in far too much green everything—Clem Applehart. As Ace—not his alter ego, the heroic Phantom Jester, so no outside help of any kind—whether magical or not.

Ace intended to survive *and* to save that certain someone, that bubbly pink-haired beauty of the wood elf race, Dazzle Sparkles—no matter the odds.

Odds that dropped drastically the moment he reached his destination for the duel.

The rope bridge dubbed the Dangling Crossing deep in the depths of Mintwood.

It swayed as awkwardly as Leaflet Peaches and her belly dancing had back as a little tween and was thrice as wide as her curved sexy slimness nowadays, a decade later.

Creaking like a horde of crickets going minstrel, the bridge drooped over its whole length of a dozen dangerous paces as if smirking oh-so-knowingly at how its planks—those logs sliced lengthwise in half—all were as red and sleek as Dazzle Sparkles' most rosy red lips at their pouty pretty smirkiest.

Least there were no obvious gaps between the log planks.

(Yet.)

But wood elves like Leaflet, Dazzle, and yes, even Clem Applehart could slip into, and slip through wood like a one of Aunt Ladle's handful of stray felines slipping through cracks. The wood itself acting like the cracks.

An ability called woodrifting.

So these half-log steps already gave Clem a big advantage.

Even if Clem only crouched on the opposite side of the bridge. Ready for an ass-kicking. Even with his dual pair of scrawny pine sabers. Sabers slightly over three feet long and nearly an inch wide at the base and for most of the blade.

Weathered pale-tan rope wove rough diamond-patterned walls that Clem could woodrift through too. Even if they seemed as sturdy as Ace's dwarven uncle, Hammer de Saber. Even as short as him too. Barely up to Ace's hips.

But same for that wannabe Clem.

And unlike that scrawny twig boy Clem, Ace was a lean and mean mountain peak of a bronze brawn. Even in dark blue slacks and bright blue vest. Long-sleeved pale-blue shirt underneath. Sleeves with some droop to them. Enough to let his hands slip underneath—if he needed to.

Since each sleeve had a slim steel dagger up it.

But here on this rope bridge there was plenty of space to topple over these low walls.

And like Uncle Hammer loved to say, the taller they grow, the harder they fall.

Since falling several paces into those raging deep depths of the azure-blue river below. Falling into the Coral River here. Worse than a hard fall.

A lot worse.

All thanks to all those gorgeously brilliant and colorful reefs of freshwater coral. The coral clung like giant lumpy boulders to the steep underwater banks of dark granite. Between those gorgeous reefs of coral was only deep dark churning rapids. No foam to hide the danger.

No sign of a bottom either.

Despite its incredibly clear azure-blue water.

Veils of steam even rose across the whole entire river. Like pale-blue curtains of thick velvet zigzagging and fluttering in the breeze. Just more of them here than in the calmer sections.

Packs of them, actually.

The smell of minced mint was even stronger too. Like the little gooey bright-green candy mints Aunt Ladle loved to make for everyone.

It was so hot here. Even up here. Several paces above the churning rapids. On top of the dark granite banks the Coral River carved a canyon through.

Banks with little room to maneuver.

Banks now mostly hidden within the azure-blue haze of Mintwood.

But Ace could handle it thanks to his daily morning routine of dragging boulders around for endurance, strength, and speed training. Hopping and maneuvering on top of those boulders afterwards to train my footwork and agility, along with more endurance.

Footwork was second to breathing in swordplay, after all.

Two decades of life and over a decade of training in the sword thanks to Uncle Hammer and his weapons classes. Uncle Hammer, after all, was a weapon master as sassy as he was superb.

Uncle Hammer even trained whole classes back at Greensap Village.

Including some of Ace's childhood friends—Leaflet Peaches. Dazzle Sparkles, and even Rosaline Applehart—Clem's sultry but sweet sister and talented witch, no less.

All three girls were amazing swordsgals already.

Even if all wood elves like them worshipped some

glowing white horses with spiral horns from the foreheads (alicorn horns they were called) and eagle wings form their backs. Unicorns or, as the girls called them ...

Alicorned Ones.

The mortal enemies of serpents everywhere—especially dragons and their ilk, from alves—basically blood-drinking serpent vampires in the form of (fake) elves—to lamias—upper half a beautiful girl, lower half a snake, and a thirst for both humans and elves, straggling them dead, that is.

Only days ago that wicked Clem had somehow wrangled a clearly unwanted agreement with Dazzle's parents, forcing poor Dazzle to marry that wretched Clem within the next few days.

Not even Clem's sister Rosaline could drag the details out of Clem, let alone Dazzle, but Ace, as Phantom Jester, caught onto some unsavory dealings with Clem's name coming up along with hints of selling a certain pink-haired beauty into slavery.

With nothing but pure hatred between them Ace challenged Clem to a duel.

Dazzle as their witness, of course, along with Leaflet and Rosaline—if their newfound duties as personal soldiers to their beloved Alicorned Ones, as Alitroopers, didn't interfere.

But Clem only agreed once Ace offered that wicked elf boy something he thought he'd never get—a chance to exile Ace from Greensap Village forever, and a sworn oath never to seek out Leaflet, Dazzle, or Rosaline ever again.

If Ace lost.

If.

But when Ace won, Clem would release Dazzle from that awful marriage agreement and never bother her, Leaflet, or let alone trouble Rosaline ever again.

So Ace had to win. Had to save Dazzle.

No matter the odds.

CHAPTER 2
DAZZLE SPARKLES

Dazzle Sparkles sighed once more. That chilly tingle down her whole entire spine. Ouchie-ouchie did she hate, no, *loathe* the cold, anything cold, like something fierce, but feeling cold?

Here?

The heat. The humidity. Hotter than boiling water. Boiling steam. So amazingly wonderful. Perfect. Refreshingly perfect. Like it always was during the late summer here deep within Mintwood.

More than hot enough for a nice quick dip. Even in hot water.

Especially in hot water like the Coral River.

So something was off. Really off. It had to be.

And not just that whole awful thing with Clem Applehart. That rotten jerk somehow blackmailed her parents, forcing them to "agree" to Dazzle into marrying Clem—no say on her part. Just do it.

In a few awful days no less!

And the Elders—useless and annoyingly stupidly agreeing with her parents.

Running off … that sounded like Dazzle's best option—after all her time at that all-girls academy, Oakengal Academy left her more than a few … options she could … pursue, and not just posing for more drawies, those magical black and white illustrations that moved based on the viewers reaction—reactions she had to pose and imitate and wow, was it fun, but also lots of tiring posing.

And just today that sweethearted Ace did the unthinkable.

He challenged Clem, that overly skilled swordsjerk, to a duel, risking a horrifying level of exile if Ace lost.

But if Ace won … Dazzle would be free again—and yet no actual reward for him but … how could she …. she ever repay him?

Even if Ace lost Dazzle would run off, and definitely find Ace and … well …

Don't get ahead of herself. Ace just might win and …

But she had to hurry. Finish her business here first. She was utterly nude and all alone at the moment. She had to be. For what she stopped here first here to do. No real choice by now but …

But what could that little nasty chill be from …

Something hidden within the depths of the azure-blue rapids of the Coral River?

This bank of black granite stretched out several paces. Like a black half moon. Submerging deeper and deeper into those azure-blue waters, but only, at most, up to her thighs. Safe and easy-going. The submerged bank. It was nice and flat and not slippery.

Much.

Perfect for a little relieving dip.

And even more so for the real reason she came here.

But no. Not yet

Not while someone, something might be watching.

The water gurgled its usual gentle echoes. Smelled as minty refreshing as mother's gooeyest mint candies and yet as watery rivery as always. Several paces over the ruffled but smooth surface of the river. Until the usual azure-blue mist grew denser and denser.

As dense as Clem never ever not taking a hint.

Except for this little secret half moon, the banks in this part of the Coral River formed a deep wide U of a canyon. Sheer pace deep cliffs on both sides. And along the sides were lodged loads of brightly colored boulders. Some like giant lumpy brains. Others like petrified bushes of small winding tubes.

All of them were various bright colors. Glowingly bright. All were freshwater coral.

Each and everyone was as sharp as the sharpest of blades.

So little chance any monster lurked in those depths.

But not no chance. Nope.

(After all Dazzle herself was here and … well.)

So whatever was watching her ... probably from behind her.

Behind her songbirds chirped their little cutie brains out. Squirrels even chitter-chattered their little rodent voices away. All within a crazy tall hedge. A hedge twice her own height of five foot eight something or other, and several times thicker. All of wild and ragged thorn bushes.

Barring the direct way deeper into Mintwood—for most.

But not a wood elf.

Or a ... clawgirl with similar abilities, when posing as a wood elf.

Just like her wood elf besties would, Dazzle already wove a few of the many palm-sized hot-pink roses into her hair. Hair flowing straight down to her waist. Hot-pink hair. For that extra yay of rosy fragrance today. Sweet and creamy and wow.

Especially today of all days ...

But still, that chilled tingle wouldn't melt away. No matter how hot the rest of her got. No matter how close she got to the edge of the river.

Her bare toes curled. As if ... reluctant to go on? Reluctant to touch that wonderfully hot water.

As if ... reluctant do what she came her for.

Up in the sky ... the azure-blue mist hide her from any spies from above. Not even the blazing sun could pierce the mist enough to show, even hint, where it was. The murky forest beyond the hedge ... even with the crazy tall hedge, some craggy oaks and crooked but slim pine tree leaned over the hedge here and there.

But only birds and squirrels were here to witness … her secret. Her other form.

The form that could, no, *would* get her hunted down, killed and and and …

Unless she … as the Ravishing Ravager … as her "real" identity and her real identity as a secret.

Heartzee would love it—and Heartzee was the key, the reason Dazzle could now transform into the Ravishing Ravager.

Heartzee was now her precious and amazingly unique hair clip on the right upper side of her hair. A living artifact, device, or something of some sort, but who knew? Shaped like a cutesy fist-sized heart, the scarlet hair clip had a pink smile and even pinker half-circle eyes.

An apologetic gift from Ace from a few years ago—not that he had needed to apologize … but a gift was a gift and well …

Ace had seemed to sad and upset despite how he saved her and her besties from the wicked warlock that enslaved them, all by threatening to kill everyone—not just her and her besties but both that warlock and himself—all in order to force that warlock to free everyone first.

Freedom she cherished ever since but now …

Now Dazzle lingered in her usual form. Her normal form. Her elf girl form. The only form her friends thought she had. Even Ace. Only her mother and father knew the truth—so far.

Unless Clem ... no, he'd never, never want her then—ever.

Since, as Ace liked to say. Dazzle looked oh-so-human and yet oh-so-stunningly-inhumanly gorgeous.

Erotically gorgeous.

The best kind of gorgeous.

The kind that made guys of all sorts see sparkles of lust for her at first glance.

An hourglass giggling to his decisive doom, whenever she sparred Ace in class, and even Master Hammer acknowledged Dazzle knew how to use her looks to her advantage. Unlike Leaflet who struggled with it, and especially Rosaline, who tried too hard to use her looks that way.

Dazzle was peach pie for the eyes. Strawberry and cream pie for the nose.

A delight to swoon every guy in Greensap—and beyond.

(As long as they didn't know the truth ...)

((And Clem didn't ruin her life in the next few days.))

But like Ace loved to say—just like Master Hammer often did too—courage conquers, cowardice kills.

So ... gulp. Dazzle ... she. She shifted.

Shifted into her lizard girl form. Her taloned lass form, as it was called by mother and father and ... others.

But most, even Dazzle herself, called her kind clawgirls.

Her peachy bronze skin stretched in place into sleek and smooth scales similar to a python. Her face down to her chest, and down to her crotch, those scales turned their natural lovely pale pink. Elsewhere her scales turned a wonderful natural brilliant hot pink.

Her hands and feet shifted too. Digits hardened into sleek talons.

Dark-pink talons.

Talons jointed, segmented like her normal digits and just as dexterous, but also extra sharp and ... savage.

Talons that let her wield her zigzaggy hot-pink lightning.

As in create it from her talons. Control it. Throw balls of it. Fire forks of lightning with it.

Even, sometimes, become pink lightning itself.

Sometimes.

Her eyes, she could feel her iris stretch. Her eyes lose their whites. And her pupils stretch into vertical serpent slits.

Her scaley skin felt tighter than usual. Too tight. So tight it would snap of any moment.

Time to molt. Shed her outermost skin. Just like what she came here to do. In secret. Super dupie secret.

So no worries, right? Right.

Dazzle was familiar with the pathway behind her. The one beside the granite banks of the river. Only a pace wide at most. Covered in straggly crunchy grass. Mostly different shades of green but some strands were scarlet. The green grass grew only as tall as her shins. The scarlet grass was as tall as her waist.

And here the layer of dead needles kept the grass at bay. From growing too dense and high, As dense and high as it got away in some of the larger clearings within Mintwood.

Denser than Clem Applehart to any hint-hint. Far taller than mother with her highest high heels on.

So ...

A watery gurgle came from behind her? Like a playful chuckle. Then smell of slimy fish, but not rotten, never again around her, at least.

Maybe that watched feeling, it was just her sweet little pack of hobgobble friends.

Dazzle sighed. Gulping.

And turned around.

Faced the captain of her secret pack of devoted hobgobbles.

A pace before Dazzle was Captain Gurgie, the mottled-blue skinned hobgobble. He kinda sortof looked a lot like what some silly bestiaries called a land octopus, or land squid. His body doubled as his head, and was perfectly round and super smooth, and was as big and as tall as her upper torso.

His head only had a mouth. No obvious ears. No obvious nose. Nope.

Nothing else but tentacles from the sides and bottom.

His wide lipless mouth stretched side to side. That happy grin. Full of a few rows of jagged triangular fangs in dark-green gums.

Yet his smile was as gentle and friendly as he could be. The same as the day a decade ago, except Gurgie was a good bit bigger now, just like how Dazzle was bigger now. A decade ago mother introduced him and his pack to Dazzle.

To serve her, her kind, as hobgobbles often loved to do.

So to see Captain Gurgie here and now ... such a relief!

Dazzle couldn't help but smile back.

Giggle too.

Lots of happy giggles together.

Even as Captain Gurgie bowed deep, like usual, his four leg tentacles were now as thick and long as her own legs and they supported his body from the grassy ground. Wiggling with excitement they crunched the shin-high green grass and bent the stray scarlet waist-high strands of grass.

His four other tenacles, two from each side, were as thick and long as her own arms and served as his own arms.

The palm-sized cushion cups along his tentacles quivered with as much excitement as Dazzle did herself.

"*M'lady,*" Gurgie said, "*May I help you molt?*"

That gurgled language. A lovely language known as Hobbish.

Only clawgirls like Dazzle and her mother could understand it so easily. Almost by instinct. It was the most common variant of the hobgobble's native languages, and why it was the language clawgirls and hobgobbles used to communicate to each other.

"*Of coursie!*" Dazzle said. "*But let's be quick! I sense ...*"

"*You sense it too!*" Gurgie said. "*Excellent! Your mother would be proud.*"

Dazzle gulped. Almost as nervous again. What made mother proud wasn't always ... fun, so to say.

"*Proud ...*" Dazzle said, "*then what ... it is?*"

"*Yes. Very proud,*" Gurgie said. "*Already proving your worth as a clawgirl. I'll explain the rest of the tests as you molt ...*"

Dazzle. Her heart.
It must have skipped a beat,
Dazzle gasped. "*Tests?!*"
No.
More than a beat.
Way more than a beat.

CHAPTER 3
ACE DE SABER

Odds that dropped drastically the moment Ace stepped onto the rope bridge.

No matter how much those half-log steps squealed and creaked along the whole wobbling bridge. No matter how much the azure-blue mist hazed most of the other side. Beyond that twig boy of a wannabe swordsman, Clem Applehart.

Least his green everything outfit made him stick out. Lime-green tunic. Uselessly short clingy sleeves of pale green. Dark green slacks that billowed near his even darker green sock boots. He even wore a green lopsided cap over his short red and overly trim dark-red hair.

Never mind the lime-green five-leafed clover over his chest. On circled with vines of gold. Real glittery gold.

Proving he was an Alitrooper. A personal soldier of the Alicorned Ones.

In other words, a fanatic.

That idiotic Clem in his green everything stuck out even more than Dazzle and her exotic hot-pink hair.

Than Dazzle going erotically gorgeous beauty in another pink-and-red undies-in-public outfit in front of the Church of the Lawful Helm—despite all the blabbering and pudgy red-faced whatnot from that Elder Priest Telltale.

Why, suddenly, the Coral River below the Dangling Crossing was, for some reason, no longer as loud ...

Despite its rapids smacking fiercely against both rocky canyon walls and boulder-sized chunks of coral jutting out of the water.

Kinda like most crowds whenever Priest Telltale pops up.

Only a couple steps along the rope bridge and the humidity grew even more intense. So intense Ace might as well be breathing boiling water. Clem must be expecting him to pass out. Or be severely weakened.

Struggling to breath.

But no.

Clem wasn't struggling at all either. Not even breaking out into a sweat.

Stranger and stranger.

But Ace breathed nice and calmly. Kept a steady heart-beat. Thanks to Uncle Hammer's latest heat resistance train-ing. Training near even hotter sections of the Coral River, and even, sometimes, in the water. Calmer sections. Water Uncle Hammer could stood on.

As in stood on top of the water.

As in standing on its surface. How he did that … more training needed to reach that stage.

Least as Ace.

As the Phantom Jester he could do things not even Uncle Hammer could manage—but no. No cheating. Not unless Clem revealed himself untrue—as Ace strongly suspected.

Too bad he couldn't just appear as the Phantom Jester but no.

Ace had saved that pair of feisty feline genie girls from slavitude as a secret weapon year ago. A weapon he now wielded, from within himself, but only with the consent of those very same genie girls, Amber and Scarlet Blaze.

Both who wanted to see Clem crushed but by Ace, not the Phantom Jester.

Not until Clem proved himself even falser than he already was.

But still, as Ace, walking up walls, or even walking on water, that technique, whatever it was called, Ace wasn't ready for it—unless he transformed into the Phantom jester.

Nor was Leaflet, Peaches, or Dazzle ready—back before they went to Oakengal Academy or even now. Not anyone in their class.

Not yet.

At least according to Uncle Hammer.

Too bad. Hopping around like some grasshopper during battle would help Ace. And if Dazzle did it too. Especially in her usual undies-in-public outfits showing off her panties more often than not … but no.

Not even Uncle Hammer could walk over the rapids below.

And the minced mint scent to the blue steam ... even sharper, sweeter now. Too strong.

Even stronger than the sections Ace trained his heat resistance.

Suspicious. Far too suspicious.

But Clem was already marching closer and closer toward Ace. Not woodrifting through the rope. Or the half-log planks. As if it didn't occur to him.

Yet.

Clem simply kept his slim pine sabers out and ready. Edging closer and closer.

As if unaware of the sudden ... oddness around them.

But Ace had his dual pair of slim pine sabers were already out and ready in his hands. Practice sabers. The only kind of weapons permitted in a duel like this.

A duel where both were meant to survive—and suffer worse by their lost.

Ace marched, wobbling with the bridge, closer and closer to Clem.

He needed more space behind him. Plenty more.

Since, as per the rules, whoever forced the other off the bridge would win the round as well and gain a point. Otherwise, the first to land a true strike would win the round and gain a point.

And the first to win three points would be the winner.

Determine the fate of Dazzle—and Ace himself too.

The rope bridge swayed from the wind smacking it from

the side. Wobbling even more as Ace and Clem both slowly and steady headed toward each other. Despite the hot wind tickling Ace's straggly dark blue hair and the sky-blue swirl of hair around his scalp.

Messy hair now.

Messier than Uncle Hammer's waist-long beard after a harsh training bout.

But Ace carefully planted each of his soft leather boots in the center of each of a half-log step. Left the bridge squeak and squeal as much as Dazzle whenever she got ignored too much.

Several paces apart they both slowed down. The center of the bridge between them. The azure-blue mist now blocked the banks of the river. The end of the bridge too. Muted its creaks and cried even more.

Bad feeling about this ... by the All Grand in Heaven—the God of All—did it feel bad ...

Worse than Leaflet pouting ultra fierce. About to smack Ace into a pancake for something he did that was too stupid for words. Something that needed correcting and quickly.

Something really was off.

Really off.

Ace knew as his time as the Phantom Jester to trust that instinct, and react to it.

But how? What was off?

No hints at what.

So how could Ace convince Clem to be .... more cautious? This wasn't a deathmatch after all. If something attacked them while dueling ...

Unless ... Clem was at the center of what was causing that off-feeling.

Clem huffed. "Come on coward. Come here for the ass kicking you so richly deserve!"

"Coward?" Ace said.

The sense that something was off showed that much?

Not good.

"Your fear is so obvious ..." Clem said. "Dazzle is mine and mine alone. You're exile is now guaranteed—exile or death, death richly deserved by my own hands!"

Uh huh. Ace edged closer and closer to that idiotically vicious Clem.

Faster and faster.

The bridge wobbling more and more.

But that smirk on Clem's sly evil face ... as he just stood there. Looking as evil as a clawgirl finishing up her latest trick on her foolishly devoted guy prey and—wait.

Sure, in one form, their public form, clawgirls looked like gorgeous human girls, or for some, even more gorgeous elf girls.

Sure, it was more than looks. They could hide and play the role of a human or elf girl for years and years.

But clawgirls were notorious for pulling tempt and trick routines on anyone from unwary travelers to even pulling the false friend routine for years, if not decades, so they were most notorious as spies and sabotage for whichever dragon they served under.

Greensap suffered their treachery more than a few times

in the past. Sabotage usually, but they were always caught by diligent dwarves and paid dearly for their betrayal of trust.

Even throughout Mintwood. Elsewhere in Trifacto as well.

Even down in the deep south. Beyond Alder Pass. Beyond the craggy mountain range. Down where demons of all kinds were hunted to the extreme. No tolerance for their existence. None at all.

Just as Priest Telltale often advised.

But the key to facing down—as Ace had done as the Phantom Jester far too often—clawgirls in their other form, their deadly lizard girl form, a form sometimes known as a taloned lass. Their skin turned to sleek snake scales. Only weak point—between their breasts—or a magical enough blade. Their hands and feet turned to talons. Fingers and toes into segmented claws.

Claws capable of a magic often unique to the clawgirl.

But in the end, facing clawgirls was the same as facing down most opponents.

It was just like Uncle Hammer taught. Drilled into Ace. And not just Ace. But everyone else in class too.

Ace tsked. "Calm wins. Rage ruins."

But Clem tsked back. "And cowardice kills."

And then vanished?!

CHAPTER 4
DAZZLE SPARKLES

Savoring the wonderfully warm azure-blue water washing over her bare legs of brilliant hot pink, Dazzle stood tall a step away from the edge of the half moon ledge of black granite, her taloned feet clinging tightly to the wonderfully hot rock.

If only Dazzle could bask like this openly. Savor the steam and heat in her taloned lass form to her fullest. After all, reptiles like her just loved the heat the mostest, right? Right.

But no. Not a chance.

Not unless she wanted to get exiled—like her childhood bestie Krystal Violetta a few years ago. All for making the critical mistake of revealing herself as a clawgirl, revealing her taloned lass form to the wrong boy—not even hurting him, just revealing her taloned lass form so that when they mate they'd become true mates and, but ... no.

That boy betrayed her. That Draven Huns. That cocky

musclehead, his deep charming voice, all too studly for a girl's own good.

And those elders. No mercy shown.

No matter how much Krystal begged and pleaded for it.

Not much different than the stray clawgirl caught by monster hunters down south. Reduced to parts used by dwarves to make weapons and armor and more.

So no.

Just because Krystal was spared her life and nothing else

…

Secret was best. Even now. Even from Ace. Her elven girl-friends—even Leaflet and Rosaline.

Especially Leaflet and Rosaline.

Even if, or when Dazzle got secretly summoned to serve some dastardly dragon overlord like all dragonborn must, eventually, often around her age too—just like mother had, and and and, but … mother found father that way—first as enemies and then …

Dazzle sighed again. If only Ace … no.

Don't ruin what they had. No.

Her molted talon-lass skin of such lovely scales washed down the Coral River. The azure-blue depths quickly sucking it under. Swallowing it forever. A true waste of a beautiful skin but … no risk, no reward didn't apply to stupid risks, after all.

Another sigh.

Dazzle took more than enough stupid risks as it was.

Way too many.

At least her beloved Captain Gurgie stayed close beside

her. Protectively, of coursie, like usual. His pack hidden for now, but definitely nearby and scouting for any potential dangers.

Ready to defend her.

His fishy smell was now so gentle, so familiar, so comforting, and never as awful as their first meeting, back when he and his pack smelled too much like rotting fish, instead of just freshly caught fishies as they did nowadays.

If only her other friends ... no.

Not even Ace would ... you know. Not if he ever discovered the truth about Dazzle. Her life, her mother's life ... maybe even father ... a disaster, even if they survived, even if they were only exiled.

But this warm water washing over her legs, washing away some of her worst worries.

And Dazzle had finally found another elf girl with hot-pink hair too. Pearl Blossom. A new drawie model too, so lots in common, even here, nearby in Greensap Village.

And even that half-elf, half-succubus Zylah Bella, she went drawie model too.

And Zylah was so gorgeous wagons crashed here and there in the street whenever she happened to walk around too wonderfully scantily clad.

Too bad none of them would ever enjoy the sight of Dazzle shifting to her talon lass form.

But maybe good too.

As good as the feel of the thick humid air against her bare scaly body. As the warm wind blowing her long pink hair.

Sigh ...

After all, the first boy she willing slept with in this talon lass form, well, she'd bond to him, as in life-long mate kind of bond, plus some magical whatnot to … to … help them both out to … well.

Poor Krystal. Her first mate-to-be betraying her … least he didn't sleep with her, or else …

Dazzle gulped.

Extra nervous gulp.

Mother promised to tell Dazzle more. Like what that whatnot actually was. When the time came, and no sooner.

(So better stay a virgin until then, yup.)

((And even more importantly: keep her clawgirl identity super dupie secret!))

(((But if she were to marry Clem, and so suddenly too … he didn't know, did he?)))

So Dazzle shifted back to her elf girl form. Her snake-like skin scales unstretching, shrinking down to such a wonderful minuscule size. So small. So much like elven skin now.

Their color changing back too, of coursie. To the lovely peachy bronze complexion everyone else knew her for and loved.

Just like her brilliant azure-blue eyes unstretched back to their elven form. White showing again. Pupils back to their regular round elven selves.

Her talons too, Reverted back to her regular digits.

Toes too.

But—ack!

Elven toes. Not ready. Unable to cling to the half moon

ledge of granite. Not against the river washing over so much of her legs. Elven legs now.

She slipped so quickly. So suddenly. Slipping down.

As if diving feet-first into the fatally fast current.

Only a yelp escaped her. A quick yelp for help.

And Dazzle.

Underwater.

Scolding how azure-blue everywhere. Gurgles everywhere. The water. Its strong minty taste. Spluttering through her nose and mouth.

While streams of bubbles wove around her. Like thin ropes. Flailing ropes. Solid and unbreakable. No matter how she twisted. Jerked herself. Pulled against them.

Struggled.

Those streams of bubbles pulled her down more and more.

Until Captain Gurgie caught her. His tentacles grabbing her securely around her chest and waist.

Her butt jabbed the the edge of the ledge. Her legs caught in the current. Her arms flailing for one more moment.

An instant later her head suddenly, but barely, pulled above the water.

And AIR!!!

Fresh clean AIR!!!

Her gasps.

Not her last.

Not by far.

The streams of bubbles. Streams wrapped around her legs. Squeezing her legs.

Shattered just as suddenly.

Washed away even quicker..

Coughing and gagging quickly, too quickly, Dazzle held grabbed Gurgie's tentacles as tightly as she did so often back years ago. Back as a little tween overdoing her adventures in Mintwood. Her life saved more often than not by Gurgie and his pack.

Like how often she foolishly trailed Ace. Even if she managed to remain undetected for so many years. Learning some of his woods guide whatnot by accident too. How he sometimes disappeared for reasons unknown and handsomely mysterious.

Since no risk ... okay, more like stupid risk but ... a girl needed some excitement, right? Right.

Dazzle giggled. but it came out as a stream of gagged coughs.

Until Captain Gurgie pulled her up even more, and then to her feet. Toward the shore. Completely out of the current. The water only washed her feet now. Nothing more.

Then, so very suddenly, he tickled her like she was a little girl again.

So her next scream. Full of joy.

Her next few gasps too. Heart still racing faster than the river current.

Until Captain Gurgie sighed. More like a sad huffie wuffie?

"Time to dress up," he said. *"your next test comes sooner than expected ..."*

CHAPTER 5
ACE DE SABER

That instant. Clem vanished. Like some slippery idiot.

No.

Crooked crook of an idiot.

Yet the rope bridge simply swayed and wobbled. Squealed and creaked like the oldest door in the Church of the Lawful Helm. Half-log steps squealing like the oldest wooden floor in the church.

No.

More like shocked goblin girls. The short rope walls creaked more and more.

The minced mint scent grew even stronger. Sharper. Too sharp to breath steadily.

Not without steady conscious effort.

Both ends of the bridge were still hidden by the azure-blue mist. Like thick cloud walls billowing in place.

Only a third of the bridge was still even visible.

The river below gurgled and chortled even louder. As if laughing at the fools fighting above it. As if its rapids were growing fiercer and fiercer. As if readying to feast on both Ace and Clem.

But how? What was going on?

Ace huffed. A little courage went a long way.

"Pathetic," Ace said.

As scornful as Zylah Belle did with her most venomous-sounding sultry voice that one time a few days ago near the Tail's End Tavern. The first time Ace ever saw that stunningly gorgeous succubus.

At how shocked he was at her utterly amazingly perfect scarlet complexion.

At her lovely black horns poking out over the stop of her head, through her long crimson-red hair. Horns upward and back kinda like curved scimitar-style daggers.

Horns lesser men hunted her kind for—and often died doing so.

At how Zylah strutted passed like an hourglass counting down to Ace's lustful stupid ...

Gulp.

No! Focus on here. Now.

Downstream and upstream ... not much more visible beyond the bridge.

Nothing beyond a dozen paces. The blue mist faded in slower, but just as thick. No veils of mist flying anywhere. Not even far away now?

And Clem could be slipping through the rope walls. Or through the half-log steps.

Aiming to slip behind Ace.

Ambush from behind.

But … no.

Too obvious. Far too obvious.

Just as a scream erupted from the wall of mist. From the side Ace faced. Down the path along the bank. Down about a dozen or so paces to the right. Deep within the mist.

That scream. A girl's scream. Echoing from a deep far distance.

And not just any girl—Dazzle?!

"AAAHHH!" Dazzle said. "Help—ACK!!!"

Ace gasped. "Dazzle!"

And he charged down the rope bridge. The half-log steps wobbled fiercer and fiercer with each and every stride. The rope walls jolted more and more erratically.

More erratic than Dazzle that one time she got drunk from "rotten" fruit juice.

More erratic than Leaflet about to collapse from exhaustion during a sparring session.

Then even Rosaline pushing herself well beyond her spell-casting limits.

Right before the bridge ended Ace. His foot. It caught something.

Ace cried out. "By the All Trickster!"

His footwork training kicked in instantly.

Ace jerked his body. Twisted backwards just enough.

But his other foot caught something too.

"Oh cursed by the All Grand!" Ace said.

No stopping it.

A yelp and Ace fell down. Hard.

Only his arms saved his face from smashing right into the ground. Into the clump of stiff sharp grass. Into the pine needles layered thickly around the grass.

Least Ace hadn't lost his sabers. They were still in his hands.

Barely.

Behind Ace Clem chuckled. As sly and sinister as always.

"A clutz and a coward!" Clem said. "You wannabe dwarf."

Then something slapped him across his ass. A wooden saber?

"Two points for me," Clem said. "And none for you!"

Ace snarled. By the All Trickster … points were only won one at a time in each round, and more, their real bout shouldn't even start until Dazzle was here, to witness their fight.

"Dazzle's in trouble," I said, "and you're—"

"Dazzle can handle herself," Clem said. "She is a skilled swordsgal, after all. Trained by your uncle, Hammer de Saber."

"Yes, but," Ace said, "that scream for—"

"I heard no scream," Clem said. "Just an excuse to coward out of our duel."

Ace crawled up to his knees. Huffed ragged.

"Then … then," Ace said, "you're worse than an idiot!"

Ace hopped up to his feet. A step charging toward Dazzle. Toward her last scream.

Until Clem struck Ace again.

Across the back of his head?!

"Another point for me," Clem said, "and none for you!"

Ace swerved around. Stumbling backwards.

"Stop you moron!" Ace said. "Dazzle's in trouble and our duel—"

Clem smirked. Eyes glinting with scornful evil. As if he savored the idea of Dazzle suffering—maybe even dying.

Or worse ... he, he really must be scheming something dastardly for Dazzle but without any real proof yet ... Amber and Blaze stayed hidden, of course, but even those two must have their limit, but ...

"Likely story," Clem said. "Three points. **Three.** You lost. Dazzle is **mine.**"

Ace snarled again. "Never you cheat! Dazzle is our *witness*! No points count without her to **witness** them! So whoever saves Dazzle—"

But Clem simply tsked loud and scornful. As scornfully as Zylah ever could.

"My step-cousin," Clem said, "just loves to play damsel-in-distress for foolish fools like you, and then turn you into a dud-in-distress."

Clem whipped one of his pine sabers toward the bridge. Pointing to the other end.

"Now accept your loss," Clem said, "and leave, leave Greensap forever, empty-handed or else ..."

But then Clem gasped speechless at who emerged from that billowing wall of mist.

CHAPTER 6
DAZZLE SPARKLES

So, of coursie, test was right.

Too right.

Veils of blue mist came upon Dazzle and Gurgie all so suddenly. Dozens of veils. Fluttering all around Dazzle and Gurgie. Thicker and thicker. Veiling them both from any eyes.

Friendly or hostile.

The heat now. So hot. So humid. Like the hottest steam baths in Greensap. The kind only earned after a hard day of even harder training in the sword, or something just as important.

More than enough to start drying Dazzle off. Kinda. Sortof. Quickly enough so that she wasn't too soakie wet. Too bad Ace, or any of the other cute guys like that brawnheaded shy-guy Jake weren't here to ogle her, but then again, if they saw Captain Gurgie, especially how tender he was with her …

No. Just no.

And unlike those steam baths in Greensap here the scent ... so minty sharp it almost hurt to breath. Kinda like whenever Master Hammer walloped her in a sparring match because she got too careless, or over-eager.

But this sharp scent even smothered the nice fishy smell of Captain Gurgie.

But Gurgie stayed beside her. Still. Devoted to the end ... if only she could find a boy that so devoted ... but no. Ace was ... devoted, devoted to all his friends, but an actual dragonborn girl? A clawgirl no less?

How devoted was he? How openminded? How ...

Dazzle gulped. The minty water of the Coral River still ... that strong aftertaste ...

Least she had to dress up, for now, before the rest really began.

Her toes curled in her platform sandals. Sandals father got for her just this very year.

Sandals of snug hot-pink leather. Scarlet soles as thick as her hands stacked on top of each other, and extra secure, especially with their low but sturdy heels, just in case she ever needed to ride a horse, or, more likely, one day, maybe, hopefully, a lamia mount.

And lamias were bottom half a snake, the upper half, elf girl ... like, so mounting one .. as a rider, a huge honor, actually, especially since few lamias humored a rider, unless properly tamed, or, more likely, compelled by their dragon overlord.

Unlike most adults, especially that whiny Priest Telltale,

her father even humored her miniskirted panties of hot-pink chiffon. Her off-shoulder bra top of more hot-pink chiffon too.

The ruby red hearts woven over each breast and her behind.

She even had the dark-pink word "Bimbo" woven as a scribble across her chest, between the ruby hearts … since so many girls, jealous girls, called her a bimbo, well, might as well embrace it, since most guys loved a girl with a sense of humor, right?

Right.

Father loved her sense of humor, and fashion too. Just like mother's back when they met decades ago. So, despite mother grimacing, well, no need to cover up too much, he often said, show it while you had it, he'd add, chuckling while mother huffed annoyed, since mother clearly still had it too, very much so …

But then, father, he'd remind Dazzle, to be careful with who she gave her heart to.

Extra careful.

And ever since Krystal … Dazzle would definitely be extra careful.

Not even Ace had her heart … completely. Not yet. No boy would. Yet. Not until Dazzle found one worthy of her trust, and …

Dazzle fiddled with her scarlet belt.

As wide as her slim hand, yet lopsided across her waist, but still snug. The chubby heart-shaped pouch weighted it down on the lower side. Stuffed full of whatnot, still, and still the same hefty weight. As heavy as a head-sized pumpkin, yet only as big as both her fists together.

And now, as these dozens of veils fluttered closer and closer, she luckily still had a slim steel dagger beside the pouch.

A steel saber sheathed in pink leather on the other side.

So she was far from defenseless.

But whatever this test was, whatever the danger, she better not underestimate it. Master Hammer trained her well enough to know that, and more.

Like not to expect the expected.

But as the mist engulfed Dazzle and Gurgie completely. Something rough and scaly scrapped the back of her hand.

She yelped. Flinched.

(All too predictable too!)

Just as Gurgie yanked her aside.

Missing a harsh gust of wind.

Dodging whatever caused that gust.

Dazzle didn't dare use her serpent sight. Not yet. No sound. No normal sight.

No telling who might stumble onto them.

Even here.

"I cannot defeat this enemy for you," Gurgie said. *"Sorry. I can only help you evade this opponent a few more times before ..."*

Gurgie yanked Dazzle aside again. Quick. Hard. Yet tenderly.

Dazzle nodded. She had two blades. Trained by the best. Near the top of the class too.

"*No worries!*" Dazzle said. "*I'll defeat it after the next dodge, he-he!*"

Master Hammer even trained her to fight with her eyes shut. He tried to train everyone to fight with their eyes shut.

But only Dazzle had managed it.

Sometimes.

Before she and some other (elf) girls were sent off to that annoyingly all-girl's academy, Oakengal Academy, Dazzle managed it only a couple of times since then. Out of several dozen attempts.

Even as the Ravishing Ravager she … she couldn't do it much, or for long.

BUT SO WHAT? No worries. Much.

A success was a success, so build off it! Fail and … well … no. No worries.

(Much.)

The mist started to whirl around Dazzle and Gurgie.

Whirl and swirl.

The scent of mint growing even stronger. Sharper.

Not much time left.

Dazzle drew both her dagger and saber. Ready to strike out at the enemy.

Using her instinct only.

No conscious senses.

None at all.

No conscious thought either. Not one bit. Just as Master Hammer drilled in her,

Into his whole entire class.

(Even if it was … years ago for Dazzle.)

So go full airhead, as she loved to say during those lessons, and only some of the girls dared to laugh with her. More like only Leaflet and Rosaline.

Last time she said it, at Tail's End Tavern, that half succubus Zylah just tsked scornfully at her.

Very scornfully.

A bit too much like the tsks echoing scornfully out of the whirlwind of azure-blue mist, and that biting touch to its smell, a lot like the awful smoke from those pipes too many dwarves loved to smoke.

Azure-blue smoke whirlwinded around Dazzle and Gurgie.

No.

Way too much like Zylah.

"Zylah?" Dazzle said. "Zylah Bella? Is that you?"

A haughty huff but then growl. A watery harsh growl.

"As if! You mistake a handsome stud like me for that slinky slut of a succubus?!"

That weirdo's voice—as watery and gurgling as any hobgobble but that Hobbish was … off, somehow. Harsher. More commanding. Less playful and admiring, and far more scornful.

So not a hobgobble, probably, then but what?

That weirdo's voice seemed to come from all directions out of the blue whirlwind around them.

Dazzle tsked. Readying to strike.

Just as a tingle chilled her whole spine very suddenly. A reaction—similar to what she felt when fighting Master Hammer years ago—and almost detecting him in time.

So Dazzle swirled. Faster and faster.

Blades out. Out like a lopsided X.

And twirling with her.

Till—CLANK!!!

The impact. Right centered within the X—where her blades crossed together

So powerful. Like a war hammer. Hefty war hammer.

Smashing Dazzle back several steps.

Shaking her up her arms. Up through her very bones.

And shivering her insides with the intense power of the impact.

An impact she couldn't keep taking much longer—despite only taking one so far.

So time for another guess.

"Really now. Too bad," Dazzle said. *"Time to die without a single kiss to your pathetic name. Such a shameful way for a—"*

"Unworthy!" the weirdo said, *"None have been worthy of my handsome tentacles! Of their wonderful suction cups! Of their hooks and—"*

Dazzle took another guess. A hunch. To throw off this weirdo more, if not anything else.

"Some arch-gobble thinks too highly of itself," Dazzle said.

After all arch-gobbles were physically similar to hobgobbles but deformed in mind and body—so definitely not handsome in any form or way—but often at least thrice the size of larger hobgobbles like Captain Gurgie—if not larger, so these attacks near her height.

Only a distraction—or a deception.

"**Some** arch-gobble?" the weirdo said. "*I am the High Arch-Gobble Knight Sir Slurpen! Knee and beg for mercy, beg and maybe,* **maybe** *your death shall be—*"

"*Awww,*" Dazzle said, "*the* **kiss** *virgin is crying. Waaah, wah,* **waaah***!!!*"

That shriek of indignant rage.

Better prepare as if about to attacked from all around her.

(OF COURSIE, a moment's thought, and obviously that wasn't where the real attack was coming from.)

No.

Suddenly streaks of dark sickly violet bled through the whirl of blue mist. All around the mist. At her height and above. More than just above.

Everywhere.

As if the swirling mist was darkening blue ink, and violet ink was spilled on it from everywhere. Too much like the artists mixing their inks. Artists that loved to draw Dazzle, Leaflet, and Rosaline in cute poses and paid them plenty.

Other elf girls too—like the pink-haired Pearl Blossom.

"*Look who's talking!*" Sir Slurpen suid. "*You-you-you ... no boyfriends no matter how slutty you dress and how giggly stupid you act and and and—*"

The violet mist grew darker and darker.

The light around them. Dimmer and dimmer.

But Dazzle stayed in place. Took a calm deep breath just like Master Hammer taught her. That sharpening smell of mint. Must be a way of hiding the fishy smell of that arch-gobble.

So, of coursie, Dazzle growled upset too—even if she felt more like giggling..

The violet mist closed in tight. Engulfing Dazzle and Gurgie.

Engulfing them so completely nothing was visible except the violet mist. The smell. Just stronger, sharper mint. The heat. Like boiling water. Hotter than any steam bath. The mist. More gooey and clingy.

But Dazzle was ready.

Her blades. Ready to strike.

Just wait for the right moment ... entice that Sir Slurpen to strike first.

And the knight's last.

"So what?" Dazzle said. *"Waiting for the right guy—"*

"Stupid!" Sir Slurpen said. *"Stupid! Stupid! Stupid! You're just another stupid clawgirl. As if that boy can be the right* **anything!** *He'll be dead soon enough. Dead! Dead! Dead! All thanks to that deal Clem made with—"*

Loud smacks rang out above Dazzle. Far above her. A dozen paces at least.

"Hush!" the weirdo knight said, *"Hush! Hush! Hush! You know too much. Time to break you. Break you long enough to repair for your sale. Sale to—"*

More loud smacks. Louder and louder.

"*HUSH!*" the weirdo knight said "*But ... so tempting to TORMENT!*"

Captain Gurgie tightened his grip over Dazzle.

But Dazzle slipped out of his grip. Moved quicker. Reacted faster.

No thought.

No thought at all.

Mind. Blank.

Body. Reacting.

Trusting her training.

Trusting her arm when it flung her dagger straight up.

Just as a gust of wind slammed down on both Dazzle and Gurgie.

A scream of shock. From that weirdo knight.

The gust slammed passed them. A gust with that sharpest of mint—and not rotten fish galore.

A loud but distant thump boomed from the ground. From out of the mist ... behind Dazzle? Somewhere behind her. Close. Far. Not sure.

Yet.

That instant. A moan. A whimpering cry. Very distant. Very gurgling.

As if the mist muffled those sounds of victory.

The weirdo knight's voice too, now, was muffled.

"*Another chance,*" the weirdo knight said, "*Just once more chance. Please. I'm ... I'm not ready to die just yet. I'll ... I'll ... if only I can take that awful Dazzle with me!*"

Dazzle giggled, and extra playfully now too.

"*Try if you want,*" Dazzle said. "*But you are so definitely going forever to the Forgotten Depths. Exactly where you and your companions deserve to go—in death!"*

Playful until another bubbly sweet voice cackled wicked right behind Dazzle.

DAZZLE. Her heart. Into her throat—it felt like. Since that voice. That wicked voice so close—despite the blue mist engulfing her and Gurgie, and and and ...

"Or so you zeenk, you little Sweet Tasty."

That nasal accent, the kind so many guys thought romantic. An accent common in the far west regions of Woodcrest Valley, where the mountains were extra high and extra cold and extra snowy.

Even further west of Woodcrest Valley too. Probably.

If stories from merchants were right.

And then the sudden strong scent of fur. Of fox fur. And of *mink*? Like ... a blend. A hybrid of sorts.

And that cold tingle down her spine. It seemed to razor Dazzle down her spine now too.

A new enemy, no doubt. One far more dangerous than any arch-gobble. Even more dangerous than Rosaline whenever she could pull herself together and fight properly.

A witch with such powerful ice-natured magic and—

"Zee Frostbite sisters shall be your doom, no?"

A second bubbly sweet voice? Beside the first. With the same cute but nasal accent.

Same blend of fox and mink fur too.

But as ice cold as Dazzle felt in her gut, as loathsome as the cold was, Dazzle giggled wickedly playfully, despite Gurgie tightening his hold on her protectively.

"Trying to even the odds? Ha!" Dazzle said, "A few new pelts? Perfect! Just what I wanted. *Right Gurgie?*"

Gurgie gurgled a cautious laugh.

"*Right,*" Gurgie said, "*as long as **they** become the pelts, not **us**.*"

CHAPTER 7
ACE DE SABER

Only moments to react. To ... to the utter shock. From out of the billowing blue mist. On the other side of Dangling Crossing.

Zylah Bella?!

And wow, was she a sexy sight! What a stunningly gorgeous scarlet-skinned beauty!

The most awesome hourglass to hellish bliss ever strutting clonk-clonk-clonk. Every half-log step got daggered by her high-heeled shin boots of sparkling black leather.

Her outfit was beyond undies-in-public. She was strapped, more like scantily clad in black leather straps. Stretchy leather. Around legs so awesome that ... that ... **gulp**, and crossing breasts that ... wow, any elf girl, even Dazzle, even Rosaline, would be jealous of that jiggling chest.

Jealous of all the attention from guys it would steal from their own.

Especially how Zylah was tall enough that her breasts were at Ace's eye level.

The perfect height. For a guy's sight.

Wow. Was Zylah like a cherry custard pie for the eyes and loins.

Yup.

And yet far better than any cherry pie Aunt Ladle could hope to whip up.

Even the wicked smirk on her heart of a face. Those big brilliant violet eyes smirking with her pouty crimson lips.

Just like the way the rope bridge smirked over the Coral River. As if in utter bliss over Zylah strutting over it. Swaying her lush hips with the sway of the bridge. Each and every movement as graceful and perfectly timed as the next.

Even her waist-long hair of wavy crimson fluttered lovely in the humid wind.

From the top of her head poked out black horns. Like a cluster of thick pointy daggers.

Horns too many men openly ogled for the wrongest of reasons.

To collect rather than admire.

Zylah was so stunningly gorgeous, and for a succubus looks matched the level of their powers, so Zylah was really strong as a succubus too.

Really, really strong. Maybe eve Phantom Jester strong, maybe.

So strong there were rumors that the highest ranked of dragon overlords, that High King Alder Kill himself, had insisted, since Zylah was dragonborn, (succubi counted as dragonborn after all,) that she serve his hordes for at least a few years.

That she serve under him personally.

Not that Ace knew her all that well but rumors he heard as the Phantom Jester confirmed that much. He'd fought succubi gone bandit as the Phantom Jester and damn, could their fire creation and control powers, crazy hard to overcome.

Let alone counter.

In her hand … a whip of what looked like braided scarlet-red flames. A whip over twice as long as she was tall, so over twelve feet long. Why its flames didn't scar the bridge. or set it on fire … more strangeness, but that meant she had far more control over it than most succubi—who would have at least scarred the wood and rope here and there.

That the whip cackled almost as much as … as …

No.

It wasn't just the whip and its flames cackling.

Zylah was cackling. Her sultry sweet voice so scornfully sinister right now …

"Surrender," Zylah said, "or die. Either way is fine by me."

Why that idiot Clem continued to gawk, mouth lower than the bottom of the bottomless Coral River, and also pointed his worthless pine saber at Zylah …

Maybe if Ace used that Clem as a meat shield while working out why Zylah was acting so strangely hostile … as scornful as Zylah was toward Ace, during their very few interactions in the past …

No. Too evil at the moment.

So better ask Zylah the obvious.

"Surrender?" Ace said. "To who? Who's your—"

"*Not* **you**, *moron*," Zylah said. "The *thing* **behind** you idiots."

Ace. His throat.

Dry.

Body frozen.

For a stupid instant. Trimming a dwarf's beard level of stupid.

Ace started turning. Before Amber and Scarlet could even try to butt in.

Zylah tsked even louder.

Clearer.

Rolling those gorgeously violent eyes of hers right at them both.

"*Don't* **you** turn around either," Zylah said. "Sheesh. How did you idiots survive so long? Ever heard of the Serpent Gaze technique? How deadly it can be? Least to you idiots without dragonborn blood in them, Honestly ..."

Ace gasped. "But Dazzle ... she ..."

"She can hold out," Zylah said, "for a few more moments ... but if you move much more ... or turn toward **that** *thing* ... not even Wizard Elder Bluerobe at his finest could save you."

The utter silence behind Ace ... the lack of any presence even ... not even a tingle down his spine from that direction but ... the strangeness of before ... the disorientating nature of it ...

Ace nodded. Pine saber up and ready—but not toward Zylah.

Until Clem snorted.

"As if," Clem said, "some hellspawn like her would ever save us!"

Zylah huffed back. "Fine. It's your funeral. Don't say I didn't try ..."

Clem growled even louder. Started raising his blade.

"Try? Try this!" Clem said. "I'll send you back to hell!"

"Stop you fool!" Ace said. "This isn't the time to—"

"**Never!**" Clem said. "Never falling for their lies **again!**"

But rather than fight outright, Ace merely blocked the idiot's eyes with both sabers.

Giving Zylah the moment she needed to flick her hand. Pulling something from behind her.

Flung that something at Ace.

A five-pointed star of crimson iron. And crimson iron was hell to anything not from hell. And that star was three or four inches wide. At least the size of her palm.

Swirling fast.

Flying even faster.

Seemingly right at Ace. His head. At eye level.

But no.

Ace didn't flinch. Didn't dare. Not at all.

Uncle Hammer trained Zylah. Trust in his uncle. If not in that succubus' friendship with Leaflet and Dazzle.

Zylah was already halfway across the bridge anyway. Soon to be in whip range.

So if Zylah wanted Ace dead ... no. No. Scorn wasn't the same as hate.

The Phantom Jester, as the one upholding a heroic creed, no

hating someone, no attacking someone without giving them a proper chance, and Zylah, she had already shown a wonderful willingness to get along with others—even elves that one day might be her enemy like Leaflet and Dazzle and Rosaline. Unlike too many succubi he fought as the Phantom Jester.

An instant later the star zipped passed Ace. Right by his ear.

And a hiss rang out behind Ace.

A thunk.

"Damn you traitor!"

Then hissed curses in some serpentine sounding language. Ace recognized barely recognized the words, but the language, a distant dialect of serpentine, a language common among serpent creatures while they did their mandatory service for a dragon overlord.

Only a pace or so behind Ace.

So deadly close and yet Ace had been so unaware of such danger ... his training. He had failed to prove it true then. In more ways than one.

But he could always improve—as long as he lived on.

Ace started turning again—until Zylah shook her head.

"She's Basil Nixie," Zylah said. "A lamia whose eye-to-eye gaze is death—unless you have dragonborn blood in you. Like I do."

Ace sighed, relieved. "Being a succubus comes in handy, sometimes."

"Sometimes," Zylah said, "but not looking forward to that dragonborn warrior crap for the next few years. Count yourself lucky you're not stuck serving either those glowing horses or the flying lizards."

With a grimace Ace nodded.

"Yeah," Ace said, "but I might get dragged in by either side as a translator at some point. I'm an All Grandest after all, so knowing lots of languages in one of my things."

Zylah sighed, grimacing back.

"So," Zylah said, "you're the All Grandest that annoying Priest Telltale keeps whining about."

Just as the sound of the thorny brush being torn through. By something that sounded as wide as a barrel. As high as his knees. Some long slither through the brush beyond the bridge.

"Spared the lamia too?" Ace said.

"Yeah," Zylah said. "I might end up serving beside her friends, you know, so now she owes me a favor. A big one."

"Good point," Ace said.

But then Clem jabbed Ace in the ribs—using his elbows, and not holding back.

So Ace. Out of breath. Painfully out of breath.

"Another point for me," Clem said. "And this time there **is** a witness to—"

SNAP!!!

Zylah cracked her whip right by Clem's idiotic head. Right in front of his eyes.

"Duel's off, you morons," Zylah said. "Master Hammer sent me to fetch you two, and Dazzle, before something bad happened to any of you idiots."

The small gust from her whip's snap. Just like cherry custard as well. But better. Sweeter. Creamier.

Helping Ace catch his breath even. Returning his breath. His heart thumping faster and faster too.

A pace from Clem, Zylah growled.

And wow, did her scarlet complexion shine so gorgeously clean and perfect this close up ... despite the intense humidity here. Or maybe, that sweatiness, because of the humidity.

"Bad?" Ace said. "Dazzle! She screamed a little while ago for help and—"

"That was," Zylah said, "the Basil Nixie trying to trick you. But since you idiots were in danger I bet Dazzle is too by now."

Ace. His throat.

Dry.

He nodded. Heart sinking.

Until Clem growled back at Zylah. His face growing a deep red. Deeper than Zylah's crimson hair. Her dark-red pouty lips.

"I ..." Clem said.

But Ace grunted. An idiot was an idiot, and no less— hopefully Clem wasn't worse. As bad as the rumors claimed.

So Ace grabbed his arm. Tight.

And using all his bodyweight behind the pull. Just like Uncle Hammer trained him.

Yanking Clem out of the way. Quick and ruthlessly.

"No time to argue," Ace said, "Right Zylah?"

"Right," Zylah said. "Maybe you aren't as stupid as you look."

"Really?" Ace said, and gave Zylah a small but genuine smile back.

Until she sighed.

Rolling her big gorgeously violet eyes away from Ace once again.

"*No,*" Zylah said, "Don't get **that** cocky."

A snap snap snap of her whip and the wooden sabers—both Clem's and Ace's—were mere ashy shatters.

The sudden fury clearly burning throughout Clem now ...

Good thing Zylah was the only one here openly armed—and Ace had hidden a pair of daggers up his sleeves.

Daggers Ace really hoped he wouldn't need to use against Clem—but just a mere hope.

Clem growled. Too quietly for his clear out-and-out fury.

Even when Zylah spoke up once again.

"Oh hush, Clamboy," Zylah said. "Count yourself lucky I'm not serving any dragon overlord yet—or else I'd have to kill your stupid ass since you are wearing that Alitrooper uniform."

"Lucky?" Clem said. "Count yourself lucky that I—"

And Clem vanished into the rope bridge once again.

"—will kill you quicker than Ace!" Clem said.

His voice. From out of the entire whole bridge now.

CHAPTER 8
DAZZLE SPARKLES

The blue mist swirled around Dazzle, around Gurgie, and whirled colder and colder. A loathsome cold. Loathsome to any reptile.

Even a secret reptile like Dazzle.

Cold enough to make Dazzle shudder. Cringe. To make Gurgie cringe even more. To shiver enough to loosen his protective grip on Dazzle.

The grass around them crackled louder and louder. From little droplets of ice forming on each strand. Covering them more and more. Ice breaking from the wind whipping the grass around.

All from some kind of ice-natured magic.

The smell of fox and mink fur grew stronger and stronger. Only one creature could both talk like that and giggle like that and and and.

Beastmites of the fox, or of the mink race, or maybe, even, a hybrid of those two races.

The giggles of those accented voices grew louder and louder. Closer and closer, and not just behind Dazzle, but all around Gurgie and Dazzle, and getting closer and closer. As if echoing from out of the whirlwind. Closer and closer.

As if less and less muffled by the mist itself.

No signs of that weirdo knight at least.

Not yet.

But maybe … that was the point. Distract Dazzle with those beastmites and let that weirdo knight strike suddenly, using surprise and whatnot.

But then the whirlwind of blue mist pulled back a few paces.

Revealing more than mere shin-high green grass, or waist-high blades of scarlet grass. Grass covered in droplets of ice. Like frozen dew in fall and spring after a morning frost.

Right before Dazzle, one of the enemies giggling at Dazzle and Gurgie.

A beastmite girl of the fox race—a foxmite.

Her huge azure-blue eyes gazed at them. Eyes as cold and blue as the whirlwind still blowing around Dazzle and Gurgie.

Her face. All too human.

Even with her pink-nosed fox snout instead of a pink-lipped human mouth and nose.

Even with her snow-white coat of short sleek fur glowing bright in the dim light.

Even with her big triangular fox ears with pinkish insides instead of human ears.

Her pale but honey-colored hair. Wedged low and far too lush. Flowing down behind her. Straight down to her overly-thin waist.

Very yankable hair, actually, so there. A fool of a fool.

But then again, beastmite girls had even better regenerative healing than genuine elf girls. So cutting her hair shorter would be pointless. It would just grow back to its natural length.

Her hourglass figure ... especially with that hefty buxom bosom and lush hips, this foxmite posed way too much in a cocky come-get-me playful flirty twist. Far too similar to an elven beauty beckoning a cute boy to come flirt with her.

Far too close to Dazzle, her own figure, her own posture, her own bubbly flirty personality.

Despite that foxmite's pawish hands and feet. They were slim enough not to be unwieldy in a fight—with or without weapons like daggers or worse.

Even with only her wickedly white and trim claws. Dangerous claws, if Master Hammer was right about their sharpness. Able to slice through lesser armor. Their cuts would be enhanced by their magical nature, in this case, cold and ice.\

Master Hammer was usually right.

More than usually.

This foxmite. Definitely a rival. In looks and more.

A rival that must, unlucky for her, die here and now.

Never mind how even her outfit was lovelier than it should be. Way too lovely.

Especially out here deep in the woods. Deep in Mintwood no less.

That stretchy-snug high-neck bra top of shiny satin. Satin as blue as her azure-blue eyes. Golden thread woven throughout it decorated it with curvy pentagrams connected with elaborate thin vines.

Its sleeves slid down to her wrists, and with gaps around her shoulders that made the sleeves stylishly off-shoulder. Sleeves just droopy enough to let her easily hide a blade, or worse, a wand with a bladed edge—a dagger wand—underneath.

That would only require a quick flick of her hand to suddenly arm herself.

If she hid a weapon under her sleeves.

Her short ruffled skirt was just as stylish. Satin as blue as her eyes. Ruffled all around. Decorated full of golden pentagrams connected by vines like her top had. The skirt reached a nice couple of inches down her thighs, and yet was as stretchy snug as her top.

And yet no hiding that a slim dagger belted around the middle of her right thigh.

And around her lower waist, a wide belt of dark-blue leather was slung lopsided over her ruffled skirt. That pouch on the lower side of the belt—same chubby heart pouch as Dazzle's, but colored a bright cyan rather than a beautiful pink.

A pair of long spiraled daggers of hung off shiny dark-blue … steel(?) hung off each side of her belt too.

"Niiiiice outfit," Dazzle said. "Quite stylish for some wild foxmite witch."

Ears perking up higher, the foxmite giggled very, very pleased, but also clearly very, very cautious of Gurgie.

Good.

No matter the race beastmites tended to fear hobgobbles. Hobgobble packs often hunted beastmite cublings, and often tween, teen, and even young adult beastmites, and successfully more often than not.

Dazzle would know. She helped her hobgobbles by luring young beastmites into chasing her—especially beastmite guys chasing her as prey, only for them to become the prey.

The prey of Captain Gurgie and his pack.

"Zee elfish clawgirl is so polite!" the foxmite said. "Zank you! If only vee did not have to fight, no?"

Dazzle giggled flirty back.

"If only," Dazzle said, "you surrender and we won't have to, true?"

"Ooo-la-la, it is tempting," the foxmite said. "You are Dazzle Sparkles, no?"

"Really? Asking my name," Dazzle said, "without giving your own?"

"True, true," the foxmite said, "Forgive me. Meeting thee one and only Dazzle Sparkles is truly exciting, no? The fame of your beauty and skill are not exaggerated. King Alder Kill veeshes to recruit you. After all you are dragonborn, no? A clawgirl hidden within Greensap."

Dazzle tsked. "Still no name? Really? Not a good first impression there."

"Ooo-la-la," the foxmite said, "you are right again. I am Snow of the Frostbite Twins. Silke and I veell be your seconds, since, if you accept now, you shall serve as a captain, our captain, but if you refuse …"

Before Snow could go on Gurgie huffed. Holding Dazzle even more protectively.

"I recognize this foxmite," Gurgie said. *"Years ago we spared her life. Her skill in creating and wielding ice was spectacular—but not enough to save her. Until …"*

"Ooo! Ooo! Ooo! I remember!" Dazzle said. "So Snow … one question before you die."

"A refusal already?" Snow said. "Alright. Zhen I shall be captain and you zee lovely lowly fodder, no? Out of gratitude I grant permission for a question—as long as it is interesting."

"Interesting?" Dazzle said. "Ha! You definitely do not remember us."

That got Snow to cock her ears, and figure even more, but Snow still widely keep her distance. Even if it was only a few paces of grass between them for now.

"Remember?" Snow said. "Remember vhat?"

"Have you," Dazzle said, "improved your desserts of slushy ice mixed with your blood?"

Snow gasped. Wide eyed and completely and utterly shocked.

But only for a moment.

The moment Dazzle needed to lunge. To strike at Snow.

At her heart—her weak spot. Plunge a blade through a beast-mite girl's heart and her regenerative healing would slow, would get exhausted quicker than from any other wound.

So this strike now.

Ending this fight before it began.

Dazzle lunged. Gurgie releasing her at the exact right moment.

Her saber plunged through the foxmite's buxom bosom. Between her breasts.

A fatal strike—if Dazzle could keep the blade there for long enough.

Except instead of struggling Snow hugged Dazzle. Strangling tight.

Just as a massive zap of pain zigzagged, radiating from those pawish hands against Dazzle's shoulder blades, shocking her whole entire body like a blast of lightning, but lighting of cold, of icy cold power.

"Niiiice strike," Snow said, "Excellent distract and strike. But alas you are now mine. A slave soldier of my squad, existing only to serve and slay whoever I veesh slain. My death shall be yours as well, but far more painful, for failing to protect me, no?"

That awful jabbing shocking pain …

"Better … die …" Dazzle said, "then live … slaved again … and … and …"

"Dazzle Sparkles," Snow said. "I order thee to spare my life, no? Remove this saber from my chest **now**."

Before Dazzle could react differently, before Dazzle could

even realize her body was reacting to that Snowball's will rather than to Dazzle's own will …

The saber was out of Snow.

Dropped to the ground.

Just like Dazzle. Kneeling before her new master.

If only she could call upon Heartzee but no. Her voice refused to call out, to summon the transformation, and turn Dazzle, free Dazzle while she became the Ravishing Ravager —a transformation that could heal her instantly. Undo any kind of curse or whatever bound her to this awful foxmite..

Snow la-sighed. "A life for a life, no? I'll forgive your treachery. Zhees time."

Dazzle gulped. No words could form in her mouth. She could only kneel.

And pray for some escape.

Some kind of rescue … but from who?

CHAPTER 9
ACE DE SABER

For a few silent moments nothing happened on the Dangling Crossing.

The rope bridge. It just waved from the humid breeze.

When suddenly the billowing blue mist suddenly engulfed Ace. Like diving into the steaming hotter sections of the Coral River—even if Ace just stood there. The humidity so thick it was like breathing hot water. Easy to get exhausted sooner than expected and pass out.

Or worse.

It even drenched his clothes soggier and soggier. His sleeves.

Good thing his daggers were on the underside of his forearm. Not easily spotted under the dropping sleeves.

The mist even smothered out every sound. Even the pounding of his very own heart.

Just sinister silence.

Until, suddenly, Zylah barked a wicked laugh—still close to Ace—and this time, not completely scornfully either.

"A deathmatch it is then, Clamboy" Zylah said. "My first kill will actually be a pleasure. Too bad Rosaline will hate me for it but war is war."

Ace gulped, almost moved in, almost went to stop them from fighting—until Zylah tsk loud and clearly at Ace.

Flying out of the mist. Standing before him. With actual bat-like wings.

Adorable black wings with crimson skin between the long thin fingers in the wings. Wings from the nap of her back. With a cute small wingspan only out to her elbows.

"I disarmed you, Ace," Zylah said, "so I'll protect you, my dud-in-distress, so keep alert. Don't get yourself killed by gawking too long at my ass or tits."

Ace nodded. "As you wish, m'lady, I'll only gawk a little."

Zylah sighed, rolling her gorgeous violet eyes again, but didn't respond to him otherwise, until a moment later.

"Back to back with me," Zylah said. "I'll trust you not get gropey."

"Ay, ay!" Ace said.

And soon they were back to back. His back in utter bliss with her soft warmth against his own back.

Almost too much bliss to notice an actual sharp dark-wooden blade streak toward his neck. Hand poking out from the rope. Flying through the rope. Gathering speed. Faster and faster.

Dodge and Zylah would die—or be hurt badly.

So Ace flicked his daggers up into his hands. Formed an X with them

Clang!

He caught the strike with that X.

And SNAP!

At the hand poking out of the rope. From the braided scarlet-red flame.

Missed.

The hand and sword had vanished once again.

But the smell of charred oak. Strong smell.

Maybe Zylah had destroyed the blade—but no doubt that Clem had hidden more than one blade here. A few blades at the very least. No. Something worse was coming.

Far worse. Clem was no fair fighter.

Something neither Ace nor Zylah could truly defend against.

And when the mist suddenly pulled back several paces—revealing that something.

More like someone. At the very end of the bridge. Between the posts holding the bridge up on that side. Now standing a few feet higher than Ace due to the dip in the half-log steps.

"Dazzle ..." Ace said.

More like rasped.

"No ..." he said. "Not like this ... no."

But no mistaking Dazzle, her heart of a lovely baby face, her brilliant lightning-blue eyes, eyes nearly glowing they were such a brilliant bright blue.

No whites.

Pupils slitted like a serpent. Freezing his foolish legs to the spot. His arms in place.

His breath.

No.

No mistaking Dazzle and her rosy pink hair down to her sexy slim waist. Her hourglass figure to heaven and back. Clothed in a stretchy snug leotard of light-pink leather, but the leather looked far too smooth and silky to be anything but human-skin leather, of even elf-skin leather.

Just like those thigh boots of dark-pink leather.

Her thin shiny bracers of pink steel. Not a single decoration on them though.

Not on her leotard. Her boots. Or her bracers.

Not even on the light-pink hood resting over her head. The light-pink cloak hanging down to the nap of her back.

"Yes💔" Dazzle said. "Yes like this💔"

Dazzle was a clawgirl. Dressed and armed like one. Her eyes confirming it.

His heart. Like a dagger went through it. All these years … pain suddenly slammed into the back of his knees. Dropping him to his knees—wobbling the bridge drastically as they crashed into the half-logs steps.

A pair of wooden blades. Dull blades thankfully, but both had came from out of the rope sides.

SNAP!

SNAP!

The wooden blade shattered into blackened ashy shards.

When Zylah suddenly cried out. In pain too. Just as icy

crackles erupted behind Ace. The chill confirming it was icy something. Near where her feet would be. Up her legs.

The chill chilling the air more and more.

Actual magical ice then.

Dazzle cackled like any wicked clawgirl would, but ... nowhere on her uniform, no a single decoration?

None.

"Lowly fodder too?" Ace said. "Really?"

More like rasped. Again. Rasping. His throat. Harsh from freezing up.

Dazzle gave him a nod? Those eyes. He didn't dare stare directly into them again but no mistaking the fear and regret and oh no.

"Really🖤" Dazzle said. "Punishment for something I did, nothing more🖤"

She reached to the sides of her thick lopsided belt of rosy pink.

A belt with a quiver on her left full of pink-feathers arrows—as if a clawgirl actually needed real arrows.

The pink-leather sheaths for a pair of scimitar-style swords, but no, she quickly drew the scimitars. Swords clearly fashioned out of bone—no doubt some human or elven—and fortified a brilliant shining pink, so as strong and durable as steel, if not better.

Their hilts a darker pink—and also bone of some sort.

Handles then snapped, linking together. Curved blades pointed outward.

Almost like a bow made of two scimitars but no string until ... there was.

A glowing thread of pink magical light. A string that could create arrows matching whatever power she had hidden from Ace, from everyone all these years.

An arrow of cackling pink light suddenly formed on her bow. Ready to be drawn and fired.

Aimed right at his heart.

On his knees—despite the wobble of the bridge—Ace had no hope of dodging—not as Ace, at least.

"So long my first love💔" Dazzle said. "And my last💔"

No scorn in her words. No. More like … a puppet than her normal self, which meant …

Wait.

Just as Dazzle started drawing her arrow of pink lightning backwards.

That hair clip Ace got her year ago. The hair clip she loved to wear everywhere.

She still had it on her right upper side of her head, in her pink hair …

Clawgirls never kept trinkets from their prey. Least none of the clawgirls he fought as the Phantom Jester. Even the clawgirls he encountered as mercenaries who hired him as a woods guide and translator and nothing more.

Valuables were also sold quickly. No attachment. Ever.

Not unless … curse the All Trickster—Dazzle must be slaved once again.

She must be.

And as Ace he had no way to save her. Not unless … unless he turned Phantom Jester at the very least—revealing his secret identity to everyone here.

Not just Dazzle but her new accursed master.

CHAPTER 10
DAZZLE SPARKLES

Moments after blue mist engulfed Dazzle completely, moments while that loathsome freezing cold ice vanished, moments after the fox and mink scent grew stronger and stronger, the mist suddenly pulled back.

More and more. Slowly but steadily back.

Even if her heart raced. Raced from her near death. Losing that fight so quickly and then ... then ... no.

No!

No!

No!

Eyes partly shut, Dazzle still kneeled helplessly, like a puppet, bowing to that wicked foxmite.

The gurgles of the Coral River. They suddenly erupted nearby. A pace behind Dazzle, actually. Splashes showered her back? How? How did she get here?

The air itself grew hotter and hotter again. Far hotter than before.

Hotter than even those notorious steam baths Master Hammer insisted all his students take right after their most hardest training sessions. Wash away the sweat and aches to better prepare for the next class tomorrow.

Melting away that last of the icy sensations from her own capture, her own enslavement.

The green grass no longer tickled her shins. A few strands of scarlet grass brushed her torso, her thighs, since this claw-girl uniform, the leotard, the thigh boots with low heels, the bracers to double as small shields that were more than big and strong enough for her reflexes as a clawgirl ...

All fashioned out of elf boy skin, no doubt. So silky smooth and stretchy snug and yet softer than soft..

Just like how her pink scimitars were fashioned out of elf boy bone of the up-and-once-coming wizard kind, no doubt.

That awful foxmite had even removed Heartzee from Dazzle and her hair. Removed it right away, actually.

Gurgie already fled too.

Best they they did. That foxmite ... no telling what revenge she'd inflict on them if they stayed.

Snow had ordered Dazzle to march this way. Keep marching until ...

Shaded in the blue mist, like a deep shadow in the haze, that rope bridge ... was it the Dangling Crossing? The very same rope bridge Dazzle was to meet Ace and Clem at and oversee the duel to determine her fate ...

As if her fate ... as if she had any control of it any more.

That's when she saw herself ... aiming an arrow of her pink lightning at ... at ...

Dazzle gasped. No.

More like tried to gasp: "Ace ♥ No ♥ ♥ ♥ "

But nothing came out. Nothing.

Since, on his knees, slumped over in clear pain, and frustration, and fury ... Ace de Saber. The one who saved her so many times before and now ... she was the one putting him in danger.

Not saving him instead.

Behind him, nearly back-to-back, was Zylah, but on her knees too. Hunched over and hugging herself. Clearly chilled terribly from the ice encasing her legs, her hips. Encasing her in azure-blue ice up to her waist.

A giggle erupted in her ear. From that wicked foxmite.

"Yes!" Snow said. "Exactly like zhees! Zylah spared her new teammate so she veell be permitted to live, as long as she agrees to serve us as she should, unlike stupid little, you who dared try to resist, no?"

"No ♥ " Dazzle said. "Ace ♥ Zylah ♥ They has nothing to do with—"

"Oh but they do, no?" Snow said. "Just like that hair clip of yours. A very *special* hair clip. Let's see how my ice clone of you handles its power, he-he."

A glimmer of hope ignited in Dazzle. Heartzee. Her last hope.

"Your scent," Snow said. "That hair clip iz your last hope! Ooo la-la-la. I suspected as much. Best not trigger it yet—not until it is examined more thoroughly, no?"

"No …" Dazzle said. "It's—"

"Who said you could keep speaking, lowly fodder girl?" Snow said. "Zhees is your punishment, after all. And vee could have been such good friends but no … trying to kill me and so quickly, no?"

Dazzle gagged. Her throat refusing to, fighting her against her own will.

Snow cackled wickedly.

"Now vatch," Snow said, "as you're only beloved idiot of a boyfriend dies by your own hand—or so he zeenks!"

And Dazzle. Now.

Really nothing she could do.

Not anymore.

CHAPTER II
ACE DE SABER

No. Don't give up. Never!

Uncle Hammer was always clear on that point.

Always.

Even if Ace was several paces away from Dazzle. A few feet lower.

Nowhere near far enough to react to her firing her arrow of pink lightning.

Especially with his knees digging down on the half-log steps. The rope sides easily within arm's reach—and even more easily within a blade's reach.

The mint scent of the humid air—even stronger now, for some mysterious reason.

But around Dazzle. Her sides especially. The mist was so thick. As dense as Ace had been to miss all the signs that Dazzle was more than what she seemed. Her stunning talent in fighting. So stunningly good she left her genuine elf girl friends in the dastardly dust.

The chills behind him. From Zylah. Her moans and whimpers. From pain. Completely.

Shivering in agony, actually, from the subtle shake of the logs, from the sound of it.

And strangely enough the mist collected down around Dazzle's feet. As if hiding something.

But not hiding enough.

Hints of azure-blue ice dotted the grass and ground. Dotted where the mist didn't completely hid it.

Weird.

Dazzle always loathed the cold. Enough that iciness by her feet—especially revealing that she was a reptile—no. Dazzle would never, no clawgirl would stand on icy ground and not even shiver, not show the slightest hint of discomfort.

Something about that Dazzle there was off..

Big time off.

Even stranger. Clem hadn't struck out at Dazzle—while striking out at Zylah the first chance he got ... that Clem stayed within the bridge, within the rope or logs, or somewhere close by ...

Was Clem Dazzle's new master?

Or in league with whoever controlled Dazzle now?

The utter silence—just the trinkle of the river below. Nothing else. Not at the moment.

More proof that idiot Clem was worse than an idiot, but a traitor.

But not enough proof—not yet.

Not unless …

Not unless Ace could drive Clem to attack the Dazzle in front of Ace. Confirm that Dazzle was fake. And show whether he's in league with whatever was causing this trouble.

So Ace tsked. "Just one last question."

"Shoot," Dazzle said, "before I do, he-he🩶"

Smirking wicked Dazzle pulled her arrow of pink lightning back—readying to fire it. No shifting her feet though—since the ice there.

Not a single crackle.

Just more and more ice gathering down there. Mostly hidden, but not all.

"Clem's your co-conspirator?" Ace said, "Or just another boneheaded—"

"I'm no bonehead!" Clem said.

That instant. From a few feet away. Clem lunged out from the post right of Dazzle.

At Dazzle.

Two more wooden blades in his hands. Raised high. Arching toward her head. Her shoulders.

And Dazzle. Her reaction time.

Slow.

Slower than Leaflet.

Than even Rosaline at her very worst.

Crackles erupting quietly around her feet. Clearly slowing Dazzle down even more.

That she had barely turned halfway toward Clem.

Twisting aside. Back. As if she'd need more space to react. to turn completely.

Just as the blade smashed into her head. Her shoulders.

Shattering that Dazzle into ... an explosion of ice and snow?

An explosion of ice and snow that flew like a wave to the left. Sweeping away the mist.

Smashing into another Dazzle the next moment. A Dazzle dressed just like that fake Dazzle had been. Now covered in ice and snow.

And that next Dazzle shrieked in shocked agony—from the cold and surprise, of course.

But behind her—shielded from the ice and snow.

A foxmite!

A snow-white-furred foxmite. Only steps behind Dazzle.

Long lush pale-golden hair hid some of her face for the moment, but not that fox snout, or those big fox ears poking out of the top sides of her head.

In an azure-blue satin bra top and ruffled short skirt. Both showed far more of her lovely figure than it managed to even pretend to cover. Both decorated throughout with pentagrams of golden threads and vines pf golden threads connecting those pentagrams.

In her pawish but slim hands—a pair of spiraled white wands with razor sharp tips.

Dagger wands.

The foxmite cried out.

"Kill zhem both!" the foxmite said. "Now! Before—"

But Ace. He knew what to do—and no hesitation to do it.

His left dagger.

Already flying toward that foxmite.

Toward her chest.

So Ace cried out himself.

"Before what," he said, "you Snowball Bitch!"

The foxmite gasped. Turned toward Ace.

Quickly.

Wands raised.

Just as the dagger plunged into her chest.

THUMP!

Her wide azure-blue eyes ... too shocked wide open.

"No ... not ... not like zhees," the foxmite said.

The foxmite stumbled backwards. Fell onto her furry fine ass.

But Ace. He was already up and running.

Running toward Dazzle.

Her legs clearly shaking in shocked agony—bound in life and death. Unless he found a way to save her—save her from that foxmite witch.

And from Clem as he crossed blades with the dying Dazzle.

CHAPTER 12
DAZZLE SPARKLES

Her legs. They were already wobbling like ... like a drunk ... like the time she snuck in some beer far before she was old enough and snuck in far too much of it. The grass tickling her below not helping. Not helping one bit.

But the pain in her chest. Like something had plunged into her chest. Her heart.

Yet nothing had.

Yet.

The ice and snow all over her. Chilling her with agonizing aches and pains. Her clawgirl uniform not powerful enough to reduce the extent of the cold, the pain, not by enough. Despite how clawgirl uniforms reduced problems from the elements. Reduced damage from any attack.

But no time.

No time to look at Ace, let alone cry out for him.

The mist was already pulling back toward her. Rushing back. The mist. Its scent. Sharp mint.

Sharper than the blades Clam lashed out at her with.

All while that awful Clem kept lashing out at her. His blades. Wooden blades as sharp as any claw. As tough as any claw—if not tougher.

Clank!

Clank!

Clank!

The best Dazzle could do was deflect each one. Bang and deflect each and every blow. Use her scimitar-bladed bow like a staff. An decorative staff rather than the bow it was. No matter how much weaker Dazzle kept getting.

Dazzle stumbled backwards. Legs still wobbling. Still weakening.

The ground. The grass. It all crackled from ice?

Ice cracking.

Shattering.

The mist … suddenly not as minty strong now?

The mist itself pulled back more and more and more.

Her foxmite master suddenly gasping even more. Struggling with her breath as much as Dazzle now struggled with her own.

Until Dazzle gasped something out herself.

"T-Time to die …" Dazzle said, "together for our … our …"

"No! D-Dazzle," Snow said. "Save me, now, and …"

"Sorrriiieeee💔" Dazzle said, "Too busy💔"

Just as Clem hammered her scimitar bow even harder. Faster.

Trying to bang it out of her hands. End her then the foxmite, of coursie.

"As if I'd like some clawgirl," Clem said, "and her foxmite master escape death!"

Dazzle giggled. Pain shocking some of her giggles.

Most of them.

"Exactly!" Dazzle said. "See Snow. We die together today."

Clem hammered Dazzle back more and more.

Snow was barely a few steps behind Dazzle now.

Less than a step or two.

Less than …

"No!" Snow said. "Silke where are you? Save us from—"

But the mist pulling back more and more. Paces behind Clem. On the other side of the post supporting the rope bridge. Enough now to reveal Gurgie. Several many steps behind Clem. Gurgie held a second Snow look-alike entangled in tentacles against the ground.

A second Snow very soon to become his next meal.

Snow shrieked. "N-N-NOOO!!!!"

"Yes 🤍 " Dazzle said. "We all die together 🤍 War is war, after allsie🤍"

Clem tsked. "Die you all will—by my blades!"

"Nopsie," Dazzle said, "and no reward for yousie, Clamboy."

Clem snarled. Smacking at the scimitar bow even harder. Faster.

Desperate clearly for the credit of her death.

"Okay, okay!" Snow said. "Mercy! I veell. I veell free you—"

just swear to save me next, and, and spare my twin sis! *Please!*"

"Agreed," Dazzle said, "but only if you both swear a binding oath to serve cute little me as well🩶"

Clem snarled. "Sadistic monsters. All of you. Now die!"

Bang. Bang. Bang.

Dazzle. One of her hands. Her right hand. It got knocked off the bow.

Too hard to grab her bow back.

Not while Clem raged against it with his own blades.

"Of course! Of course!" Snow said. "Hurry Dazzle. Before … before …"

The agony in Dazzle, in her chest—it suddenly vanished!

Her strength—returning.

Her speed. Her agility. Restoring.

Just as her bow got smacked from her other hands.

Clem snarled, smirking in victory. One blade, its tip, pressed between her breasts.

The other tip. Against her neck.

"Time to die," Clem said, "you pink-haired—ack!"

Ace!

He tackled Clem down from the right! Crashing him into the ground. To Dazzle's left.

But an instant later Clem sank, then vanished into the grassy ground.

But Ace. He stood up.

Faced Dazzle and the confusion—a dagger in his right hand, but not toward her. Since the hesitation in his eyes … his whole entire body …

Until Dazzle did what she should have done ages ago.

She kissed Ace. Right on the lips. No holding back.

Not at all.

And all that confusion, hesitation in his eyes. It all vanished instantly.

Especially when he returned the kiss in full.

CHAPTER 13
ACE DE SABER

Heart still thumping in a ravished rush from that kiss of lifetime, Ace could only still stand there, in the tall ice-covered grass, staring into the billowing azure-blue mist of Mintwood, holding hands with Dazzle, while those two foxmite witches worked on repairing all the harm, the damage they had caused.

Like freeing Zylah from their ice while healing her too.

Even if the mist was too thick once again to keep an eye on them, the mist covered half of the Coral River before them, hiding most of the colorful freshwater coral too.

But Dazzle, her confident, and comforting grip on his hand, she clearly was using some kind of magical bond to enforce their good behavior for the moment. The very bond those foxmite witches used against Dazzle—from the sound of their words before.

No doubt once they earned her trust those foxmites might regain their freedom.

Maybe—assuming Dazzle would be allowed to release them.

No telling with dragon minion crap.

Behind them the wall of brush loomed above them. Full of pink fragrant roses. Roses Ace helped Dazzle tied into her hair here and there. No worries about the future—yet, but soon enough ...

Least Ace hadn't agreed to serve either those flying lizards or those glowing horses.

Yet.

But eventually Dazzle might be forced to fight her elven girlfriends Leaflet and Rosaline, and her other friends she made at that all-girls academy. A fight Ace couldn't stop unless he went Phantom Jester at the right time and place— and figured out a way to stop the fight without getting either of his friends in deeper trouble.

Trouble as deep as the Coral River was here.

Those azure-blue depths gurgled and splashes as loudly as that strange big hobgobble Dazzle kept calling Gurgie but ... as spine-tingling as its presence was, if Dazzle trusted it, he'd trust it too.

Least the hobgobble stayed back. Deep in the mist. Keeping an so-called eye out for any trouble incoming.

And with Clem escaped ... no doubt blabbering about Dazzle and her clawgirl nature ...

Sigh.

Trouble was definitely coming, sooner or later.

"You sure you won't return to Greensap?" Ace said. "I'm sure Uncle Hammer and Aunt Ladle will stand up for you. It's not like you sabotaged anything. And with Zylah, and those foxmite witches, you—"

Dazzle kissed him silent.

Almost as silent as the misty world around them.

Almost.

"If I go back," Dazzle said, "it'll be that Alitrooper's word against mine and who do you think the other elders will believe? Nearly everyone else too?"

The damage to the bridge was almost all gone too. Thanks to those talented foxmite witches.

All those half-log steps were perfectly fine once again. The rope unharmed as well.

"But ..." Ace said. "Least give them a chance."

"A chance to prove," Dazzle said, "my worst fears true?"

"Or you're worst fears false," Ace said.

And he squeezed her hand tenderly. Hoping beyond hope that she'd give everyone else a chance but ...

But Dazzle clearly only gulped too nervous to actually agree.

Yet.

No doubt now—there was only one way to avoid her leaving now and forever and ... unlike the mysterious mist here in Mintwood there was no mystery about what he'd need to do here and now or risk losing Dazzle forever.

So, as calm and determined as the Coral River here before them, it was time to man up and ... and ...

CHAPTER 14
DAZZLE SPARKLES

azzle did her best not to cringe at the thought of leaving so quickly but ...

The Coral River was as deep as the trouble she'd soon be in if she stayed. The mint scent was as sharp as the fury soon directed her way. Even with the nice pink roses tied here and there in her long pink hair to ease her thoughts but no.

Least the last of those awful icy tingles were long gone. The grass underneath her feet was nice and soggy soft. No more icy crunches or crackles. Just simple soft smooth ground now.

Snow and Silke. The Frostbite sisters. They had been the source of those tingles.

Now stuck serving Dazzle the same way they tried to force her to serve them,

Least for now.

Least for a while—until Dazzle could trust them not to try slaving anyone else again.

The Dangling Crossing should be fully repaired soon enough. No hint of damage anywhere. So harder for Clem to claim the worst.

Maybe.

But Ace ... he held her hand tenderly but ... sure the whole harem with Dazzle on top might nudge him to claim her for the wrong reason but ... sigh. Ace wasn't like that, was he?

Clem was. No doubt about it.

Some other guys too.

But not Ace but ...

The blue mist was glowing brighter and brighter. Warmer and warmer. As if the Coral River was heating up the place even warmer. Steamier.

Scented Steam bath style.

Maybe she'd show Ace that nice little place for them both to bath in but ...

It was nearby, after all, maybe a few several dozen paces downstream or so, and so a little funsies in her elven form with Ace shouldn't be a problem, especially now that he knew the truth about her, and well, they were adults now so a little physical funsies ...

No problem at all.

Right?

Right.

So ... yet .. .her own heart raced silly at the thought since

... first time, and well ... it's not like he ever saw her taloned lass form yet, but ... well ... the steamy hot azure-blue water might be the best place to show how nice a clawgirl could look hot, naked, and scaley, he-he.

So ...

Ace suddenly slipped his arm around her waist?

Side-hugged her so sweet and tenderly and warmly and ...

"I'll," Ace said, "I'll be your mate, if you'll have me, and, well, if you stay, since, well."

That ... well ... her heart seemed to stop, for a moment, since, well.

Dazzle side-hugged Ace so tenderly back.

"Maybe I will have you, he-he," Dazzle said, "but Leaflet and Rosaline ..."

"Will understand," Ace said, "or ..."

"Or what?" Dazzle said, "you'll help me harem them as you know, my best friend nibbles? They're both gone so Alitrooper that ... no much choice other than to you know ... see who claims who as ... you know, and well ..."

"I'll figure something out," Ace said. "I always do."

"Yeah ... you always do," Dazzle said, "and this time, I'll help you out too. Maybe a little girlfriend-to-mate tournament. Winner gets you, and be head of your harem-to-be, he-he."

Ace gave her the sweetest perverted smirk ever.

"Lucky me," Ace said. "I—"

Dazzle pecked his lips quiet again.

"Nopsie🤍" Dazzle said, "Lucky me🤍 A clawgirl finally finding such an understanding and trustworthy guy who—"

This time Ace kissed Dazzle quiet.

And this time Dazzle didn't break off the kiss. No. She kept it going.

On and on and on.

About the Author

Widely traveled, Jonathan Evan Hudson spends as much time studying life as he does writing gripping tales of fantastic adventures. From the giant redwoods of California to the deserts of Israel, his thrilling stories all draw on first-hand experiences and expand them with the fantastic and his acclaimed creativity.

Be the first to know!
For the updates and more:
www.JonathanEvanHudson.com

youtube.com/@jonathanevanhudson
tiktok.com/@jonathan.evan.hudson

A War Of Lust And Oak

Read Now!

The Elf Girl Effect

Read Now!

The acclaimed Jonathan Evan Hudson once again weaves an unforgettable tale brimming with spicy page-turning action and fast-burning enemies-to-lovers passion.

Meet the newly knighted Roo Vorshaya. Sworn to protect humanity in the isolated mountain town of Appleharth. Dreams of action-packed adventure and passionate love under a lovely but sinister strawberry-pink sky.

Love re-ignited by a whiff of the familiar peaches and cream scent of his long-lost childhood girlfriend: the notorious elven witch Amber Peaches.

And endangering everything Roo holds dear.

Love page-turner novels of epic fantasy? Love reading from dusk to dawn? Then go read *The Elf Girl Effect* now!

Martial Art Of The Phantom Saber

Read Now!

SUCCUBUS SLASH

The acclaimed Jonathan Evan Hudson weaves an unforgettable tale of thrilling action and adventure spiced with fast-burning romance and doused deep in epic fantasy.

Enter Miles Mayhem. Rich in friends and enemies. And a fat boy badass in the sword.

A seriously delicious smell of bacon and eggs smothered in spiced razor-hot cheddar signals celebration—and serious trouble ahead.

Trouble beyond anything Miles ever expected.

The perfect epic fantasy novel. A genre-enlarging feast for fans of sexy action and fabulous adventure. Read *Succubus Slash* now!

Sword Master Of Honey Heart Resort

Read Now!

Into Shadow Forest

Read Now!

A diamond in the rough the bestselling Jonathan Evan Hudson weaves a thrilling tale from explosive beginning to satisfying end in the awe-inspiring land of Grandcrest.

The talented twenty-something sword master Romeo Bladell yearns for love and adventure.

And at the musty edges of Shadow Forest. Near the towering high oaks bearded like stout old dwarves. By a canyon like a wound gnashed deep through in the granite. A canyon like the maw of a stone dragon.

A strange unexpected rope bridge hangs silently. Sinisterly.

Beckoning adventure—and danger unimaginable.

Enter *Into Shadow Forest* and savor the most spectacular of page-turning epic fantasy novels. Love unique monsters, riveting battles, and fantastic femme fatales? Then read *Into Shadow Forest* now!

Angels Of The Sword

Read Now!

Crossing Of Shadowed Death

Read Now!

The acclaimed master of fantasy Jonathan Evan Hudson once again shines through with his talented story-telling. Time to enter another stunning awe-inspiring world of dangerous demons, magical mayhem, and action-packed adventure.

A simple demon-hunting mission. The young and lonely Dirk yearns for amazing adventure, for gorgeously under-dressed dancer girls among the towering high ferns. Among the even taller pines of the hot and humid Fern Shadow Forest.

Pine needles everywhere. And so fragrant they made the finest of teas.

Sturdy reliable cobble roads of the Divine Empire cut through the whole entire forest. Providing the only safe passage.

Or so Dirk thought ...

Enjoy this sexy, action-packed epic fantasy adventure from the talented Jonathan Evan Hudson. Love to read an enthralling epic fantasy novel full of stunning rip-roaring battles with creative new monsters? Then go read *Crossing of Shadowed Death* now!

A TASTE OF INTO SHADOW FOREST

A diamond in the rough the bestselling Jonathan Evan Hudson weaves a thrilling tale from explosive beginning to satisfying end in the awe-inspiring land of Grandcrest.

The talented twenty-something sword master Romeo Bladell yearns for love and adventure.

And at the musty edges of Shadow Forest. Near the towering high oaks bearded like stout old dwarves. By a canyon like a wound gnashed deep through in the granite. A canyon like the maw of a stone dragon.

A strange unexpected rope bridge hangs silently. Sinisterly.

Beckoning adventure—and danger unimaginable.

*Enter **Into Shadow Forest** and savor the most spectacular of page-turning epic fantasy novels. Love unique monsters, riveting battles, and fantastic femme fatales? Then read **Into Shadow Forest** now!*

CHAPTER 1
ROMEO

Romeo Bladell knew there shouldn't be a rope bridge crossing the canyon here yet ...

Here it was.

And the canyon itself was a deep jagged gash in the granite. Actually, more like how the maw of a deep gray dragon was.

(Not that he'd ever seen a dragon of any sort, but maybe one day ...)

The canyon itself was only a few good times wider than he was tall—but he wasn't exactly tall, and now that he was in his late twenties, it was long past the time where he'd get any taller.

The posts the ropes were tied to were stout logs. They only went up to his knees, but they still reminded him of his stout dwarven grandpa, whose bald head, even when he was on his toes, could only reach the tips of Romeo's chest.

But ... the logs looked older than some of the thick craggy oaks behind him. You know, the kind of oaks so old the moss of them doubled as old guy beards.

No, dwarf beards.

The planks were light gray and as warped as the weird joke the world had to be playing on him. The occasional gust of wind was refreshingly cool, like a lemonade during a hot summer day—like today actually, it was hotter than a hot spring with a roasting rock tossed in, so the gusts were more than welcome.

Each gust also made all four ropes of the bridge crackle out as loud as the crows in the bearded oaks behind him.

The bridge was even sunken a bit by the middle.

Like a sly bridgy smile—at the joke being played on him.

He was a lean and mean five foot six, so yes, he was a bit on the short side, for a human, but compared to dwarves, he was on the taller side, and he was muscular enough to wear his red jerkin like a vest, with no shirt, and his brown slacks were snug, but not tight.

Rather than risk another pair of flimsy sandals breaking again, he went with his reliable suede boots. They were dark red and the darkness was not entirely from the dirt of use. They were like thick reliable socks. Thick enough to protect his feet yet he could still easily feel the soggy soil underneath them.

Feel the few smooth pebbles in the soil.

Maybe climb down the canyon but ... the sides of the canyon were steep cliffs. At the bottom it would be incredibly slippery. It would take another hour or two. No. More like three. Assuming the light lasted. Longer if it didn't.

Much longer—and for what?

His backpack was basically a big bag with shoulder straps. It was made from sturdy burlap but far from water proof. It had some long-awaited precious books—more than a few of those books were the latest dime dreadfuls meant for guests, but he got to read them first to ensure there weren't any obvious problems. There were more than a few bottles of absolutely needed olive oil for lamps and cooking. Most important of all, some general provisions for the next few days.

Get the provision wet ... and not just the books ... yikes.

But Romeo ... the hackles on his neck stood up just looking at the odd bridge. It seemed to promise the hope of saving him over two hours. The usual bridge was an arch of stone along the paved usual road, but it crossed the river below long after the canyon was no longer a canyon.

And that bridge was well over another few hours hike away.

This shortcut, hiking along the canyon already saved him a few hours since the regular road made a very wide curve around the forest behind him.

All because rumors of monsters in there, but they were just rumors. Yup. Still, the bearded oaks behind were a part of the fringe of what was known as Shadow Forest and he had seen some of the corpses of the beasts in there ... like horse-sized blue jays called jumping raptors and ...

No.

They and the other dangerous beasts were only found much further south, much deeper in the forest, not here, in the fringes, at the edge of the civilized world.

In fact, that hint of danger was a draw to the Honey Heart Resort. Honey Heart Resort was a spring bath inn and resort on top of the mountain here where Romeo was working at for the past few years.

Sigh.

So as Uncle Jethron would say, trust your nose when all else fails, and Uncle Jethron was among the best trackers in the county—human and dwarf.

So ...

CHAPTER 2
ROMEO

... Sniff. Sniff.

The smell ... earthy soil. Mossy oak like all forests everywhere. The cool crisp clean smell of the river below. Echoes of the splashes and crashing of foamy rapids splashing against unyielding rock. Echoes snapping against the canyon's steep sides.

The usual smells. Sounds.

The midday rain had washed away his own footsteps from the morning trip. The crazy heat had already dried out the soil enough for it not to be outright muddy.

Just damp.

In fact, the wooden posts showed the usual expected grim from the ages.

You'd think the bridge had been here for ages too.

But it hadn't.

This very morning, on the way to town, back when the taste of his latest experimental pine needle tea was burning his mouth far too bitter, there hadn't been any rope bridge here at all.

Along the cliff on the other side of the canyon, the lichen showed no scraps along the jagged rock cliffs—no sign of any climber involved in setting up the bridge.

And Romeo read enough books over the years to know what's involved.

Rope would of been secured on one side of the canyon, and the climber climb down, go cross the foamy rapids by jumping the slimy slippery rocks, and climb up and stake the ropes on the other side.

In fact, Romeo had done such work as a side job here and there.

Another, more straightforward approach was to shoot arrows with rope tied to the ends into one of the trees beyond the canyon. Someone else on the other side would then tie the rope to the post.

Or if a heavier rope was needed, only a lighter rope would be shot and secured to the trees on both sides of the canyon. The thicker rope would be carried over and tied to posts on each side.

But ... no matter how much Romeo studied the line of bearded craggy oaks on the other side, there wasn't a sign of torn moss, of any arrows shot into their bark, or even a sign that the dirt was disturbed in the slightest.

Looking up at the sky, mostly blue with some clouds, but ... less than a few hours to sunset.

Legends said monsters were most active after night, and this close to Shadow Forest ...

Getting to the road ... he might not make it back in time.

Aunt Tilda would. be. *pissed.*

She was as big as ma, being her older sister and all, and she was the kind of women a guy would sprint a few laps around, as a woman should be, would be what pa would say, and grandpa, but ... ugh.

He really to get back before sundown.

Aunt Tilda was the boss lady of Honey Heart Resort, and he knew there were more than enough provisions for the night. For the next morning ... enough. Aunt Tilda could scrap enough together to last a couple more days but ... sigh.

Lucky for him it was Tuesday, not Monday. Tuesday was the slowest time of the week, even now, during the peak of summer, the hottest and busiest season.

But Romeo also knew this path wasn't commonly taken. Few even knew of it. Most travelers would take the long winding road rather than risk whatever trouble the fringes of Shadow Forest may throw at them. Rumors of monsters and worse things ...

Sigh. Would Aunt Tilda believe him about this bridge?

Even if she did, she'd absolutely forbid him from taking any "short-cut" (or "long-cut" as she'd call it then) off the road ever again.

(One sister and his foolish hubby lost was enough, she'd say, she wasn't about to risk her dear nephew, the last of her flesh and blood ...)

And ... honestly, it's unlikely anyone else would even run

into this rope bridge. No other witnesses. This place was so ... empty ... so ... weird ... weird place for a trap but deep down ...

112

WANT MORE?

Go to

WANT MORE?

Go to

www.JonathanEvanHudson.com

www.ingramcontent.com/pod-product-compliance
Lightning Source LLC
Chambersburg PA
CBHW030818200726
48288CB00004B/1288